The
Abandoned
Lighthouse

The
Abandoned
Lighthouse

By Albert Lamb

Illustrated by David McPhail

Roaring Brook Press/NEW YORK

Text copyright © 2011 by Albert Lamb
Illustrations copyright © 2011 by David McPhail
Published by Roaring Brook Press
Roaring Brook Press is a division of
Holtzbrinck Publishing Holdings Limited Partnership
175 Fifth Avenue, New York, New York 10010
www.roaringbrookpress.com

Library of Congress Cataloging-in-Publication Data
Lamb, Albert.
    The abandoned lighthouse / by Albert Lamb ; illustrated by David McPhail.
— 1st ed.
      p. cm.
    Summary: A bear, followed by a boy and his dog, use a rowboat to float to
an abandoned lighthouse where they all spend the day fishing, cooking their
catch, and then joining together to make the lighthouse work again.
    ISBN 978-1-59643-525-4
    [1. Lighthouses—Fiction. 2. Boats and boating—Fiction. 3. Bears—
Fiction. 4. Dogs—Fiction. 5. Friendship—Fiction.] I. McPhail, David,
1940- ill. II. Title.

PZ7.L1597Ab 2011
[E]—dc22

2009042734

Roaring Brook Press books are available for special promotions and premiums.
For details contact: Director of Special Markets, Holtzbrinck Publishers.

First Edition 2011
Printed in March 2011 in China by South China Printing Co. Ltd.,
Dongguan City, Guangdong Province

1 3 5 7 9 10 8 6 4 2

To Willa and Molly
—A.L.

For Matthias, drummer in the family band,
and true Down-Mainer
—D.M.

The bear often came down to the beach to stand by
the freshwater pool under the waterfall and wait for
fish to come tumbling down.

One day there was a rowboat on the beach. It smelled good. The bear had eaten a good fish supper and felt like a nap, so he lay down in the boat.

The tide came in. The rowboat floated out to sea . . . with the bear in it.

The next morning the boat came to rest on the rocks below an abandoned lighthouse.

The bear found lots of good fishing in the rocks,
but the rowboat floated away.

That evening a boy was playing on the beach with his little dog, kicking a big ball around.

The rowboat was stuck in the sand at the edge of the water, and the boy accidentally kicked his ball into the back of the boat.

When he climbed in to get his ball, the rowboat floated
away. The little dog barked from the beach and then
jumped into the water and swam out to join the boy.

Eventually the boy and the dog fell asleep and
didn't wake up until morning.

By then the rowboat had perched itself on the rocks under the abandoned lighthouse once more.

The bear had spent a lonely night in the bottom
bunk of a bunk bed up in the lighthouse keeper's
room, and he was glad to see the boy and the dog.

He showed them his fishing technique and they cooked the fish in the stove upstairs.

Then they all ate fish.

That night the little dog slept on the big table in the window. The little boy slept on the top bunk and the bear on the bottom bunk.

The winds blew and a storm grew. There was
thunder and lightning. The little dog was scared.

Suddenly the little dog saw a huge ship out on the ocean, lit up by a bolt of lightning. Then he barked as loud as he could.

The boy and the bear jumped up and saw the ship
coming toward them out of the storm.

The boy climbed up into the light room at the top of the lighthouse and lit the nine wicks of the giant oil lamp.

The bear helped the boy push the heavy reflecting
mirror into position so their lighthouse light would
shine on the ship.

When the captain of the ocean liner saw the bright light he steered his ship away from the rocks. The boy and the bear were so tired that they went straight back to sleep.

But the little dog kept looking out of the window at the storm until he couldn't keep his eyes open any longer.

When they woke up the big ship was gone and the
sun was out. They went downstairs and the rowboat
was bobbing among the rocks.

The boy got his ball and they all piled into the
rowboat and headed out to sea.

It wasn't too long before the bear was wading in his
favorite pool under the waterfall,

and the boy was kicking his ball on the beach for his little dog to chase after.

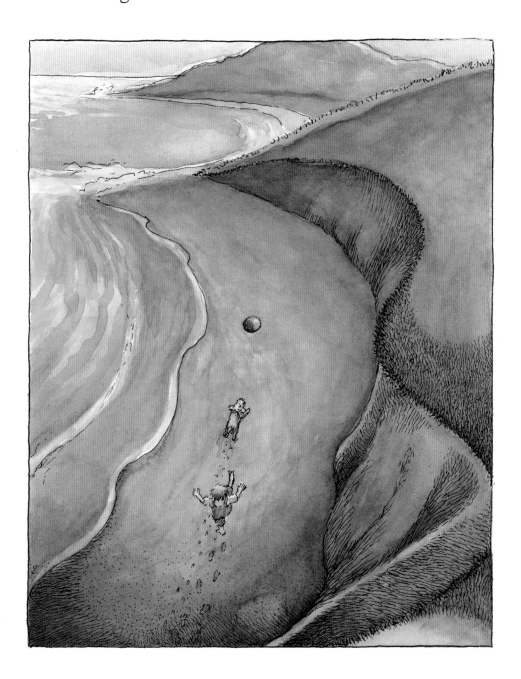

Far down the coast the big ship was being pulled
into its harbor by sturdy tugboats.

And out on the ocean the rowboat was floating
away and away.